Playground

D1512352

For Deborah
~ D B
For Maddy
~ E F

LITTLE TIGER PRESS
1 The Coda Centre, 189 Munster Road, London SW6 6AW
www.littletigerpress.com
First published in Great Britain 2000
This edition published 2005
Text copyright © David Bedford 2000
Illustrations copyright © Elaine Field 2000
David Bedford and Elaine Field have asserted their rights
to be identified as the author and illustrator of this work
under the Copyright, Designs and Patents Act, 1988
Printed in China • LTP/1800/0451/0612
All rights reserved • ISBN 978-1-84506-336-8
2 4 6 8 10 9 7 5 3 1

LITTLE TIGER PRESS
London

It's my turn!

by David Bedford

illustrated by Elaine Field

Oscar and Tilly found a playground.
"Shall we play on the slide?" asked Oscar.
"I'll go first," said Tilly.

"I'll go now," said Oscar.
"Not yet," said Tilly.
"It's not your turn."

"That looks fun,"
said Oscar.
"Is it my turn now?"
"Not yet," said Tilly.

Tilly went round and round on the roundabout.
"Is it my turn yet?" asked Oscar.
"No," said Tilly. "I haven't finished."

Tilly went round
and round
and round
and ROUND . . .

"I feel dizzy," said Tilly.

"This is fun."

"I feel better now," said Tilly.
"Can I slide after you?"
"No," said Oscar. "It's not your turn."

"Can I go on the swing after you?"
asked Tilly.
"No," said Oscar. "It's still my turn."

"Get off, Tilly," shouted Oscar.
"It's my turn on the see-saw."
"The see-saw doesn't work," said Tilly.
But when Oscar jumped on the other end . . .

Then Tilly
came down
and . . .

Oscar went up . . .

WHOO

Oscar and Tilly
played together
all afternoon.